Hey Kids!
keep your eyes open to find all the mistakes and all hidden gold coins.

This seat belongs to
Zemirah

We race to class to hang our gear. I place my lunch box in its place and take my seat to start the day,

Now its story time as teach would say, we clap, we cheer, we all hooray.

but it seems I've made a big mistake.

Thank you guys for everything,
you help me to do better,

A C B
D F E G

Write the correct
order

We eat our lunch, we take a break,

It's recess time we rush to play.

We run, we jump,

we laugh, and color

we head back in to learn our numbers.

I jump for joy to show my page

Oh ok, now I see. I thank you guys for helping me.

1 3 2
4 5 9
7 8

Write numbers in correct order.

It's great we all help out each other
but now it's time for shapes and colors.

A triangle, a rectangle, my favorite shade of pink.

Draw a triangle, 2 squares, rectangle and circle.

I raise it up and ask the class to tell me what they think.

We pack our things and head back home. Oh what A day I'm very proud, , I clapped, I smiled, I read out loud.

Tell Gabby about a time you learned from a mistake.

SUPPORT EVERYTHING GABBY

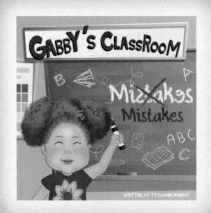

COMING SOON

←

Made in the USA
Columbia, SC
31 October 2022